IT'S S COLD ON THE PRAIRIES...

WIT & WISDOM
ABOUT WINTER

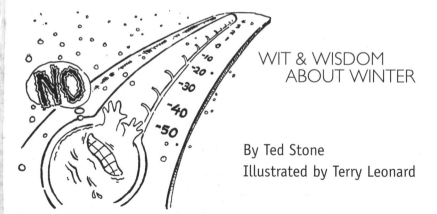

By Ted Stone
Illustrated by Terry Leonard

The Publishers
Red Deer Press
56 Avenue & 32 Street Box 5005
Red Deer Alberta Canada T4N 5H5

Credits
Cover and text design by Terry Leonard
Printed and bound in Canada by Friesens for Red Deer Press

Acknowledgments
Financial support provided by the Alberta Foundation for the Arts, a beneficiary of the Lottery Fund of the Government of Alberta, and by the Canada Council the Department of Canadian Heritage.

COMMITTED TO THE DEVELOPMENT OF CULTURE AND THE ARTS

THE CANADA COUNCIL | LE CONSEIL DES ARTS
FOR THE ARTS | DU CANADA
SINCE 1957 | DEPUIS 1957

Canadian Cataloguing in Publication Data
Stone, Ted, 1947–
It's so cold on the Prairies
ISBN 0-88995-218-3
I. Title.
PS8587.T673I7   1999   C813'.54   C99-910345-8
PR9199.3.S76I7   1999

Introduction

No people on Earth talk about the weather as much as people from the prairies. Almost every conversation begins with, "Cold enough for ya?" They cheerfully bundle up their children and send them out to play in temperatures that people in warmer climes would call abusive. They go shopping and leave their cars running for hours at a time. You'd think auto theft would increase, but who wants to go out in a prairie winter just to steal a car? It's been said there may be fewer drive-by shootings on the prairies simply because people don't want to roll down their windows.

On the prairies snow can fall almost any month of the year. Winters are so cold school children really do freeze their tongues to metal posts. Blizzards sometimes rage across the landscape for a week or more.

But prairie people take it all in stride—in boots they buy not just for size but for temperature rating. They nod smugly to each other when three inches of snow virtually shut down cities to the south.

Global warming? El Niño? Prairie people might pray for it, but deep down inside they don't believe it. They may bask in the sun through a shortlived summer at the cottage, but they know winter's out there—it's waiting for them.

–TED STONE & TERRY LEONARD

P.S. Don't forget to plug in your car.

Temperature Conversion Chart

Californians arrive on the prairies wearing parkas and long underwear, hoping to find out what cold weather is all about.　　**40°F / 4°C**

Californians refuse to go outdoors.　　**0°F / −18°C**

Californians ask to be placed in storage.　　**−10°F / −23°C**

Californians can't figure out how to plug in their cars.　　**−20°F / −29°C**

Californians consider abandoning their cars so they can fly home.　　**−30°F / −34°C**

Californians look frantically for a little something to take the chill off, but everything has frozen in the bottle.　　**−50°F / −46°C**

Californians peak out from under their bedcovers, just a bit.　　**−60°F / −51°C**

for the Climatically Challenged

40°F / 4°C	Prairie people talk about the unseasonably warm temperatures—no matter what the season.
0°F / −18°C	Prairie people spend more time outdoors because the mosquitoes have died off.
−10°F / −23°C	Prairie people begin thinking about taking their winter coats out of storage.
−20°F / −29°C	Prairie people plug in their cars.
−30°F / −34°C	Prairie people consider closing their summer cottages for the season.
−50°F / −46°C	Prairie people notice the weather getting a bit chilly.
−60°F / −51°C	Prairie people close the bedroom window, just a bit.

It's so cold on the prairies that politicians keep their hands in their *own* pockets.

9

It's so cold on the prairies that a hot idea is just a pleasant fantasy.

11

It's so cold on the prairies that
at least once every winter the
temperature drops so low the entire
population tries to escape to Arizona.
But by that time it's so cold nobody's
car will start.

13

It's so cold on the prairies that by the time your car warms up you've already arrived at the place you're going.

15

It's so cold on the prairies that when the temperature hits −40°F (−40°C) people sometimes cheer up because the weather's getting warmer.

In 1887 the temperature at Ft. Keough, Montana, dropped to −65°F (−54°C), setting a continental U.S. record that lasted 66 years.

17

It's so cold on the prairies that joggers breathe out the sides of their mouths to keep from bumping into their frozen breath.

It's so cold on the prairies that even snowmen wear long underwear.

21

It's so cold on the prairies that
when people talk about a cold snap
they mean the loud crack the air makes
when the mercury plunges lower than
−40°F (−40°C).

On January 24, 1916, the temperature in southern Alberta dropped 100°F (38°C),
from 44°F (7°C) above to −56°F (−49°C) in just 24 hours.

23

It's so cold on the prairies that *everybody* wears balaclavas when they go into a convenience store.

Langdon, North Dakota, holds the U.S. record for the most consecutive days below 0°F (−18°C)—41 days from January 11 to February 20, 1936.

25

It's so cold on the prairies that a
pot of boiling cowboy coffee will freeze
while it's still sitting on the campfire.

27

It's so cold on the prairies that matches lit outdoors freeze faster than the wind can blow them out.

29

It's so cold on the prairies that lakes freeze solid from top to bottom and then shatter into small pieces when the weather turns really cold.

31

It's so cold on the prairies that dogs have been known to freeze to fire hydrants.

On January 20, 1954, temperatures in Montana plunged to an all-time low of −70°F (−57°C).

33

It's so cold on the prairies that even your shadow won't go outside without a coat.

It's so cold on the prairies
that even snow geese wear
down-filled parkas.

It's so cold on the prairies that the snow sometimes covers entire houses and people have to shovel paths to their chimneys so the smoke can get out.

During an average winter in Canada, one septillion snowflakes fall: that's 1,000,000,000,000,000,000,000,000.

It's so cold on the prairies that February is considered the longest month of the year.

41

It's so cold on the prairies that three-day blizzards blow in every two days.

A ten-day blizzard in southern Saskatchewan ending February 8, 1947, left a Canadian Pacific train near Regina buried under a half-mile long snowdrift that was 25' (7.5 m) deep.

43

It's so cold on the prairies that sometimes the mercury won't even come out of the thermometer bulb to register a temperature.

45

It's so cold on the prairies that birthday cakes are always frosted.

A single cup of snow can contain more than one million snowflakes.

47

It's so cold on the prairies that a hot flash is just another term for summer.

49

It's so cold on the prairies that sometime around Christmas the cows start giving ice cream and frozen yogurt.

It's so cold on the prairies that if you turn around quickly you can sometimes catch your shadow jumping up and down trying to stay warm.

On February 15, 1936, Parshall, North Dakota, was anything but partial to its record-setting low of −60°F (−51°C).

It's so cold on the prairies that even the man in the moon won't come out.

55

It's so cold on the prairies that spending the summer at the cottage only takes about a week.

It's so cold on the prairies that on quiet nights you can hear the trees shiver.

It's so cold on the prairies that politicians go the entire winter without speaking. Most years they never say a word before April, and it usually takes until the middle of July before they build up enough hot air to give a full-blown speech.

61

It's so cold on the prairies that even the icicles huddle together on the south side of buildings so they can warm themselves in the sun.

63

It's so cold on the prairies that when a blizzard blows in, chickens have been known to lay the same egg twice.

65

It's so cold on the prairies that
there are only two seasons:
winter and road construction.

It's so cold on the prairies that by the time you get your kids dressed to go outside at least one of them will have to go to the bathroom.

In Tower, Minnesota, on February 2, 1996, the mercury fell to a record low of –60°F (–51°C).

It's so cold on the prairies that you get nine months of winter and three months of bad cross-country skiing.

It's so cold on the prairies that the last frost of spring sometimes doesn't occur until after the first frost of fall.

It's so cold on the prairies that the term hot-cross buns refers to a common mix-up where two people try to back into the same fireplace at the same time.

It's so cold on the prairies that by the middle of February stories about how cold it is no longer seem humorous.

77

It's so cold on the prairies that people try to break into prisons—not out.

It's so cold on the prairies that some nights people have sex just to survive.

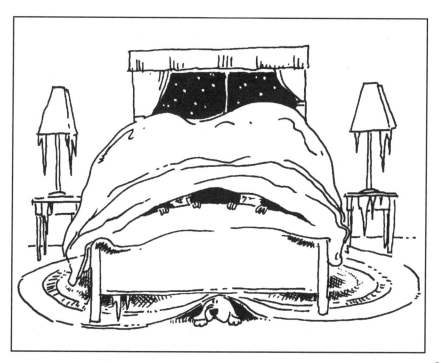

81

It's so cold on the prairies that by the time people remove all their layers of clothing, they've forgotten they wanted to have sex.

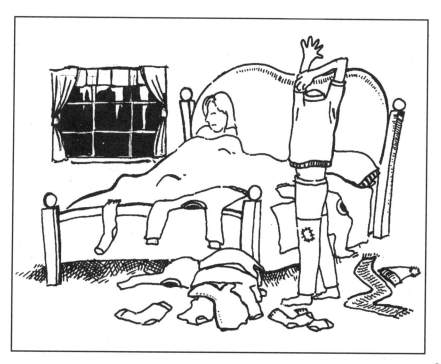

It's so cold on the prairies that people's dentures keep chattering after they've been taken out.

On February 12, 1899, Camp Clarke, Nebraska, recorded its rock-bottom temperature at −47°F (−44°C).

It's so cold on the prairies that
Victoria's Secret should have a special
prairie edition catalogue featuring
sexy thermal underwear.

It's so cold on the prairies that when someone says "log on" in an office full of computers everybody thinks the fire has just been stoked.

It's so cold on the prairies that
people put food in their refrigerators
to keep it warm.

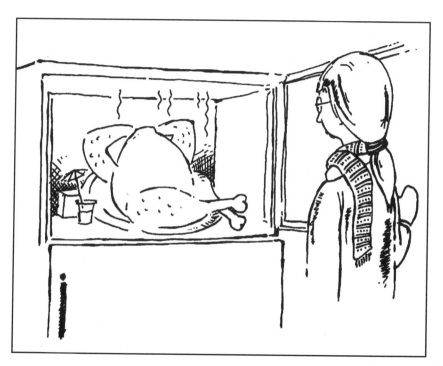

It's so cold on the prairies that when climatologists refer to "mean winter temperatures" people don't realize they're referring to "average."

It's so cold on the prairies that people do one of two things: hibernate or migrate.

95

It's so cold on the prairies that houses
really do go bump in the night.

It's so cold on the prairies that even nudists wear several layers of clothing (which is far less than most people).

It's so cold on the prairies that
people have heated arguments
just to stay warm.

*The lowest temperature ever recorded in Wyoming was at Riverside R.S.
when the thermometer read –66°F (–54°C) on February 9, 1933.*

It's so cold on the prairies that your newspaper is never hot off the press.

103

It's so cold on the prairies that when people say "See you in the spring," they really mean "See you in Palm Springs."

It's so cold on the prairies that politicians are happy when their escapades land them in hot water.

It's so cold on the prairies that even teenagers sometimes put on coat.

109

It's so cold on the prairies that
money is always cold, hard cash.

It's so cold on the prairies that cold shoulders are what everybody cries on.

On February 17, 1936, McIntosh, South Dakota, saw the mercury plummet to −58°F (−50°C).

It's so cold on the prairies that cabin fever is welcomed as a way to warm up.

It's so cold on the prairies that
the size of funerals always depends
on the weather.

It's so cold on the prairies that *everybody* bets the groundhog will see his shadow on February 2, but there's nobody out to take bets.

119

Don't miss Ted Stone's other national best-seller:
Cowboy Logic: The Wit and Wisdom of the West

"Never piss into the wind or drink downstream from the cattle."

"The meek shall inherit the earth—but they won't get the grazing rights."

"Never cry over spilt milk—it could have been whiskey."

Here are more than one hundred sayings from a cowboy lore that is rich in wit and down-on-the-ranch common sense. Guaranteed to keep readers chuckling page after page after page.

"A feisty volume of sayings . . . that'll keep you sounding like a genuine cowpoke till the doggies get rounded up and come home." *–Monday Magazine Humor*

ISBN 0-88995-152-7 paperback
128 pages • 5 1/2 x 4 1/2"
B&W illustrations throughout
CDN 7.95 • US 6.95 • UK £4.99